Kohn and Kohn

by

Marie F.T. Boyle

This is a work of fiction. Names, characters, businesses, places, events and any incidents described are the product of the author's imagination or are used in a fictitious manner.

Any resemblance to actual persons, living or dead, or to actual events is purely coincidental.

To my friends and extended family who
gave me encouragement and help in writing
and publishing this book.

4

Prologue

"If you offer your food to the hungry and satisfy the needs of the afflicted, then your light should rise in the darkness and your gloom be like noon day"

-      Isaiah 58:10

6

Part One

It is Christmas Eve 1966 and a heavy fog is hanging over London. This is not unusual or unseasonal but, for many, it is utterly inconvenient. Airports are closed and flights cancelled. Passengers by the Irish Ferries are experiencing high seas as the great waves toss back white manes of glistening foam. Passengers by the channel ferries are more fortunate and are actually experiencing calm seas with not a puff of wind. Two passengers in particular are trying to reach London before Midnight. Isaac Kohn- a merchant banker is travelling from Dublin. His brother and partner in business is travelling from Zurich. They have arranged to meet at Victoria Station. It is not because of Christmas that they are anxious to reach London before midnight. The Kohn's are Jewish and Christmas is not their feast. They are rushing to the bed side of their nephew Benjamin Kohn - the only child of their only brother Adam who are both partners in the London branch of Kohn & Kohn.

Fritz Kohn is in a pensive mood as the channel ferry ploughs her way towards Dover. He has been in Zurich a long time now - married there many years ago and is now widowed. Since his wife died two years ago he has felt a longing to be back in London. He has no children to fill this void in his life and has become a rather lonely man.

At last they reach Dover and are soon speeding through Kent in a rather crowded London bound train. There is a sense of an English Christmas in the air with beautiful houses nestling among orchards and farms. Fritz marvelled at how prosperous Kent has become in the past twenty years.

The train was due soon at Victoria Station and friends of the passengers who had come to meet the train stood behind the porters. Soon the great engine loomed out of the fog which hung more thickly over the Thames. Fritz and Isaac Kohn came face to face. It was quite a few years since they had seen a yellow London fog or heard the rumble of the city which is music to the ear of a true Londoner. Isaac described his experience in the Irish channel as beastly as the ferry was lifted high but rapidly receded and ploughed her way towards Holyhead. "It was a scary experience he said." However, they were here now and very pleased to see each other.

They had booked into the Madison Hotel and decided to go there right away as it was too late to visit the hospital, even though they knew Adam and his wife Rachel would be sitting by the bed side of their dying son. Grief for the stricken parents was only part of their concern. Their bank, Kohn & Kohn, had been left in a mess with no heir to take over were anything to happen to Adam. Benjamin had been expected to take over the Bank that their father Fritz built up when he came to London from Hamburg after the First World War. Now Benjamin was dying. Isaac and Fritz had already decided that they must persuade Adam to sell his shares and Benjamin's to them.

This was really the purpose of their visit and they both knew that they were going to have to fight an uphill battle.

As Rachel Kohn sat by the bed side of their dying son her heart was almost at breaking point. While she waited for her husband Adam to come from work her thoughts drifted back to the night thirty years ago when Benjamin was born. Adam had sat by her bedside while she drifted in and out of consciousness after a caesarean operation. He was so happy and proud of his beautiful son. They had been married five years when he was born and had almost given up hope of ever having children but at last here he was, an 8-pound boy, with red hair and blue eyes. This was a surprise really because both Rachel and Adam were very dark. Rachel was French and until her parents came to visit her she would not know how far back the red hair went in the family. The Kohn's were all very dark for generations. All these memories were going through her mind while she waited for Adam. She recalled the day, thirty five years ago, when as a young medical student she went to watch a tennis match at Wimbledon with one of her friends and left her wallet in a telephone kiosk. It was quite some time before she missed it. When she went to the police she was pleasantly surprised to find out that a very honest gentleman who was also going to the match found it. The police gave her his telephone number as she insisted that she must ring him up and thank him personally. Just at that moment Adam Kohn walked in the door on his way back from the match to enquire if anyone had claimed the wallet and was introduced to Rachel Guerin. It was love at first sight. After a whirlwind romance they became engaged and in less than a year were married.

They encountered a few obstacles in that year. Adam was a Jew and Rachel a Catholic. Adam's two brothers and partners in their bank Kohn & Kohn did not approve of the marriage as Rachel was twenty years younger than Adam and her being a Catholic made them look upon her less favourably. However, they weathered the storm and were soon settled down and happy in Adam's home in Regent's Park. Rachel recalls those halcyon years when love was new and they had travelled a lot. She had been born and lived most of her teenage years in the picturesque village called Carennac in the Dordogne in south west France. She always went to Carennac for her holidays while she was a student in London and intended to return there when she qualified. However, when she met Adam she knew that London was the place she wanted to be. He was everything that she wanted in a man – dark, handsome and kind. When she finished her studies she decided not to pursue a career in haematology so she would be free to travel with Adam when he visited his other banks in Zurich, Paris and Dublin. Haematology was the branch of medicine in which she was interested but she decided that now was not the time for more study. Perhaps some time at a future day she thought.

Five years went by and Rachel was beginning to give up all hope of having a baby. She knew that Adam would have liked an heir but in all those years he never showed any sign of disappointment. His brothers on the contrary made things very difficult for her at times. They had no children of their own and on the few occasions when they met one would imagine that it was her fault that Kohn & Kohn had no heir. There was a slight improvement in their relationship when Benjamin was born and she had consented to have him brought up in the Jewish faith. They actually gave him a substantial amount of shares as a gift. Rachel recalls how happy Adam and herself were in those far off days. He never refused her anything.

Up until the beginning of World War II, when Benjamin was three years old, he brought them to Carennac in the Dordogne where Rachel was born and brought up. Adam loved this village - described as one of the beautiful villages of France with its delightful jumble of honey coloured stone houses with brown tiled roofs clustered around the old priory. He loved to walk around the village of narrow winding streets and historical buildings - some dating from the 16th century. This delightful blend of half-timbered houses leaning at crazy angles and grand turrets enhanced by window boxes made it look like a Cotswold village in the sun. During the war years when they did not go to France Adam brought them to the Cotswolds because it was so much like Carennac.

When Adam was twelve and ready for secondary school his uncles Isaac and Fitz hoped that he would go as a boarder to Eaton. However, Adam and Rachel had chosen another school for him near their home where he could attend as a day pupil. It was a Catholic school with a very good reputation. His uncles objected on the grounds that, despite its good name, this was a Catholic school and not suitable for a boy of the Jewish faith. Adam argued that if Rachel was kind enough to have him brought up as a Jew the very least they could do was to allow her a choice of school. After a while, his uncles succumbed to Adam and Rachel's wishes and Benjamin was enrolled at St Gabriel's Oratory. They had made the right choice they felt. He was very happy there and met a few boys of the Jewish faith who became his lifelong friends. His uncles worried that when the time came for his choice of wife that he may follow in his father's footsteps and marry a

Catholic. Rachel could read their thoughts so well.

Things took a turn for the better when he got a place in Oxford to study Law with a view to joining the family bank. His uncles were very proud of him and again gave him a substantial amount of shares in the bank which pleased Adam and Rachel very much. Those years which Adam spent in Oxford were a very happy time for all of them.

When Adam was twenty three he joined his father's bank in London and also spent some time with his uncles in Zurich and Dublin. He showed great promise from the start and by the time he was thirty was a great asset to the firm. He was now established in the London branch and lived with his parents in Regent's park. They were very pleased with his choice of friends who he brought home quiet frequently. They enlivened the lives of Adam and Rachel. They did not travel as much now but they still loved to visit Carennac where Rachel's parents still lived.

One year while Carennac was enjoying an Indian summer and Rachel and

Adam enjoying an extended holiday there Benjamin came to see them and dropped a bomb shell. He told his mother first that he had been diagnosed with pancreatic cancer and, being a doctor, Rachel knew that her son may not have long to live. Together they broke the news to Adam who was utterly shocked and kept saying "it can't be, it can't be". His world has been shattered and Rachel knew that in spite of her own heart break she would have to keep strong for Adam. These thoughts were all going through her head as she sat by Benjamin's bed side and waited for Adam. Her son had been in a coma for weeks Suddenly she thought she saw his eye lids flicker. She called a nurse who came with a doctor. He went to consult a senior doctor. The nurse also left the room for a short period leaving the patient's notes on the bed. Rachel had a peep at the notes and was horrified to find that they had written his blood group as AB on the notes. Rachel herself was 'O' blood group and she knew that she could not possibly have a child that was AB. She pointed this out to the nurse when she returned and said that the hospital must have made a mistake. The nurse was not pleased that she read the notes but knew that she should not have left them on the bed. She also knew that she would have to tell the doctors about the incident when they returned as Rachel seemed very agitated. Soon Adam entered the room and was upset to find his wife distressed. The doctor assured them that they would do everything in their power to get to the root of the problem.

That night Benjamin died with Adam and Rachael by his bedside. They tried to console each other but they knew that life would never be the same again and that the years ahead would be empty and lonely. Benjamin's many friends from St. Gabriel's Oratory and Oxford University came to join his many friends from Kohn and Kohn Bank to pay their last respects. His two uncles Isaac and Fritz were very emotional. Not only had they lost their only nephew but they had also lost their heir to the bank.

After the funeral they all assembled at Adam and Rachael's home for refreshments. Benjamin's many friends gave Adam donations of money to give to his favourite charity. Adam and Rachael were very touched. The immediate family then waited a little longer for the reading of the will. Isaac and Fritz had assumed that Benjamin would leave his shares to Adam. They were shocked to discover that he left them to his mother Rachael explaining that as she had consented to having him brought up in the Jewish faith and had sacrificed her career to look after him it was only fair that she should be rewarded. Adam wasn't at all surprised because Benjamin had told him this when he made the will and he had agreed. Fritz and Isaac were furious. It meant that Adam and Rachael now between them had the majority of shares in the bank and Rachael was still a young woman. They must persuade Adam to sell his shares to them. They would wait a little while till the dust had settled before making any suggestions.

In the meantime, the hospital had been in touch with Adam and Rachael to confirm that Benjamin's blood group was indeed 'AB'. Rachael's blood was again checked and it was confirmed that she was group 'O'. Their worst fears were confirmed - they must have been given the wrong baby in the hospital where he was born. It was explained to them that if they wanted to get details of all the babies born in the hospital on Benjamin's birthday that they would have to go through a legal procedure and that it was usually a lengthy one and sometimes ended in heartbreak. Rachael sobbed on Adams shoulder and said

"Benjamin was my son and I don't want any other son. From now on I want to live with my memories of him. If my baby was given to some other woman he is probably very good to her and why should I spoil that?" Adam took her in his arms and kissed her. Somehow he felt that she was speaking words of wisdom.

Weeks went by and at last Isaac and Fritz came to see Adam at the bank. He knew when they called that it wasn't a social visit and they very soon got down to business. Isaac spoke first and explained that in the interests of the bank they would like if he signed his shares over to them so that they could look after Rachael in the event of anything happening to him. Fritz explained that his wife had no son now to look after her and as she was still a young woman they wanted to make sure that their combined shares didn't fall into careless hands. Adam sat motionless. He couldn't believe that his brothers and partners could be so callous. No way was he going to leave Rachael - the love of his life - to their mercy. Benjamin had done his best for his mother. He would do the same. He had a good few years left in him he hoped. He rose to his feet and quite calmly informed them that he already had plans for his wife's future. He thanked his brothers for their concern before escorting them to the door.

As Adam emerged from the tube at Green Park Station on his way home he decided to sit for a while in the little garden where he sat so often in the past. It held so many memories for him. It was here that he proposed to Rachel and it was here that she broke the news to him that they were expecting a baby. This evening he was in a very pensive mood. He felt that he was in a very bad place after meeting his brothers but he was determined to rise above the occasion. He was not going to let them interfere with his private family life. He didn't interfere with theirs. Rachael was now his only concern. Sitting on his special seat he marvelled at the peace of the place. It wasn't long before he was joined by another man who seemed to be a bit down on his luck. He was carrying a black plastic bag that contained something like a sleeping bag. He soon began to eat his tea on the park bench as if he had no home to go to. He offered Adam some of his crisps. The gesture touched Adam profoundly. Here was a man who had so little offering to share the little that he had with a stranger on a park bench. It was in sharp contrast to what he experienced earlier on when he met his brothers. He declined the crisps saying that he had already eaten but thanked him most sincerely for his kind gesture. They got talking and Adam soon learned that the man sharing the seat was indeed homeless.

"I once had a home" he told him "but when my wife died I was not able to look after my son so they took him into care". He added that the drink got the upper hand of him and he ended up on the streets. "But you do not smell of drink today and I noticed that you are drinking coke" replied Adam. "I gave up the drink years ago said the man, "but it is hard to get back to where I was at my age. Tonight I will sleep here on this bench beneath the stars and by midnight, if I am lucky, the Methodist mission will bring me a carton of hot soup and words of comfort. God is very good to me - I never go to sleep hungry. Now that is enough about me" he added. "You look a bit sad yourself sir if you do not mind me saying so. You have lost some one near and dear to you too and you are now worrying about someone else that you love"

"Are you a fortune teller" asked Adam, quite stunned by what he had told him. "No not quite" said his friend, "I am just someone who gets glimpses into the future and I like to help people who find themselves in a bad place".

"You have been very kind to me this evening by talking to me and I would like to help you. If you let me hold your hand Matt Malone will tell you things that will surprise you" Adam very reluctantly gave him his hand.

Matt closed his eyes and explained to Adam that he had no need to worry about what would happen his wife when he died. "She will be very well looked after by your son and grandsons and a Jewish lady called Miriam...Miriam. I see a famous building, I hear music...music, I see flowers, and the beautiful lady called Miriam. Matt Malone can see no more but go in peace because these things will come to pass, my friend" he said.

When Adam rose to go he pressed a bunch of notes into Matt's hand and gave him his business card. "Ring me in a few days" he said. "I might be able to find you a place to stay".

"God bless you" said Matt. "I will pray for you".

Adam had been in a very pensive mood as he emerged from Green Park

Station and made his way through the hustle and bustle of a London rush hour to his home in Regent's Park. Somehow a peace had enveloped him – a peace that he hadn't experienced for many months. 'Surely' he thought to himself, 'I can't find myself believing in Matt Malone's prophecy. He said that my wife would be very well looked after by my son and a girl called Miriam. How did he know that I have a son? He said that he wasn't a fortune teller but he would appear to have the gift of prophesy' Adam continued to ponder. 'Perhaps I have a son somewhere out there' he thought, 'who needs me as much as I need him'. These thoughts were going through his mind but then he remembered Benjamin's face and the love Rachael and himself had for him. Rachael was right, he could never be replaced in their hearts. He remembered her exact words, "If another woman had been given my baby he is probably very good to her so why should I spoil that?" 'Yes, Rachael was right. I must put these thoughts out of my mind. Benjamin was my son and now he is gone. I will be resigned to life without him' he thought. But deep down he hoped that Matt Malone would ring up and give him new hope.

When he entered the house Rachael was in the kitchen cooking their evening meal which was always very special in the Kohn household. He gave her a hug as usual. They had grown very close again since Benjamin's death. She noticed this evening that he looked quite serene and thought that perhaps he was beginning to get over his grief. Adam was determined not to tell her about the encounter with his brothers earlier in the day or indeed his encounter with the homeless man on the park bench. He decided to let things take their course. Rachael was in a very good mood herself that evening. She had decided to give away Benjamin's baby clothes that she had kept stored in a trunk in the attic all these years. She felt that some other woman might appreciate them. When she told this to Adam his face lit up because he felt that she was healing just as he was. It would take time he knew but it would happen eventually. Still, those niggling thoughts kept coming back. Have I a son out there?

Next day he made an appointment with his solicitor and asked him to set the wheels in motion – he was going to look for his birth son. He felt guilty about not confiding in Rachael. He had never kept any secrets from her before but this time he felt it was best not to hurt her while she was still grieving.

After months of waiting they got a letter from the hospital solicitor. It would appear that all the boys born in the hospital on the day of Benjamin's birth were black with the exception of two – Benjamin and another baby. When the solicitor wrote to the other baby's home address the letter was returned 'not known at this address'. The solicitor wasn't in a position to release the name but Adam and himself were determined not to give up until all avenues were explored. It was going to be a lengthy process.

One day in the office Adam got a surprise telephone call from Matt Malone thanking him for the money he had given him in the park and asking him if he knew that there were two fifty pound notes in the bundle. Adam replied "Matt, I never counted that money. It was given to me on the day of my son's funeral by family and friends to give to my favourite charity in memory of him. I put it into my jacket pocket and forgot about it until I met you. I hope it brought you luck because you have changed my life more than you will ever know," said Adam sincerely.

"I'm glad to hear that" said Matt, "because the money that you gave me brought me good fortune as well". He further explained that when he left the park he went for a shower and a shave. He then went into a charity shop and bought some nice clothes. He changed in the shop and when he looked at himself in the mirror he couldn't believe what he saw – he was his old self and felt very good indeed. He hadn't felt like this for years. It was getting quite late so he decided to try a men's hostel in Abbey Street and ask for a bed for the night. As luck would have it who was in charge of the hostel only an old friend who worked with him when they were both steel erectors on the Isle of Grain Oil Refinery. Dan Molloy was an Irishman known affectionately as

'Donegal Dan'. He had an accident on the job and was never able to do steel erecting again. He had got compensation but had to find light work for the rest of his life. Dan and Matt were so pleased to see each other again after all these years.

Very soon Dan had got Matt a bed and they talked about old times late into the night. Dan remembered well the day on the Isle of Grain when the police came looking for Matt to tell him that his little seven-year-old son Mattie had run away. Matt hadn't turned up for work that day and didn't ring in. He hadn't been doing very well since his wife died. He was drinking heavily and found it very hard to look after his son who was grieving for his mother. Mattie was very unhappy with the woman who was looking after him and he ran away several times. Usually he was found quite close to home but this time he would appear to have gone further afield. Eventually the police found Matt Malone lying in a drunken stupor in Ashdown's Alley near his home in Strood. He was not able to help them. It was obvious that he had been drinking for days and the police suspected alcoholic poisoning and had him admitted to hospital. Matt was in a very bad place indeed.

Meanwhile the search continued for his son Mattie who had been missing all day with no money. It was getting quite dark and the police and search party feared the worst. At last a phone call came through to the police that a little boy had been found by a woman walking through the Rochester cemetery. He was sitting on a grave eating buns and drinking lemonade which was later found to have been stolen from a local shop. He would appear to have been crying a lot. Mattie Malone was sitting on his mother's grave – his world in tatters. That night he was admitted into care. A new phase in his life was about to begin.

Next day social services informed his father Matt, who was in a psychiatric hospital, that they had found a foster home for Mattie with a Methodist minister and his wife who had no children of their own. It was only a temporary measure until he got on his feet again. They were willing to bring Mattie to see him but Matt didn't want his son to see him in hospital and told them that he would rather wait until he was fully recovered and able to bring him home again. He thought of Mattie all day and prayed for him well into the night. He had a strong Methodist faith from his Welsh upbringing and he knew that his son would be well cared for in a Methodist home while he was recovering. Sadly, his hopes of getting home were dashed when a severe depression set in. It was going to be a long time before Matt was ready to leave hospital. He decided that it was best for Mattie not to see him although this decision was causing heartbreak to both of them.

He had poured out his heart to his old friend Dan Molloy who was determined that from now on he would give him any help he could. Donegal Dan had always had a generous spirit.

Meanwhile Adam and Rachael were slowly being healed of their grief. Adam had gone up to the attic and resurrected the baby clothes from the trunk. When he was emptying the trunk a piece of paper fell on the floor of the attic. On it was written 'Mary Keown, 44 Church Street, Camden'. He brought the slip of paper downstairs with the clothes and showed it to Rachael. Memories came flooding back to her. Mary Keown was the girl who was in the twin bedded room with her in the hospital when Benjamin was born. They had great fun together. She was Irish and very pretty with red hair. They often joked about her having the same coloured hair as Benjamin. Her husband was dark and their baby David was dark like his father. The day they were leaving the hospital they exchanged addresses and promised to keep in touch but alas they never did. Rachael wondered what became of Mary and her baby.

Adam was in a pensive mood. He had detected the similarity between the two names – Keown and Kohn. 'Could some mistake have been made?' he thought. At last he had a lead which he had every intention of following. He felt guilty about not telling Rachael but he was determined to do this on his own – even his solicitor must not know. Rachael was going to Carennac for a few weeks so he was going to explore the only lead that he had.

After Rachael had left for France Adam went to the given address in Camden. A black lady answered the door when he rang. She was not able to help him as they had only just moved into the area. They consulted the people next door who were elderly. They weren't much help either, but as they were speaking another lady came to speak to the elderly couple. This lady told him that she used to live on the road many years ago and remembered an Irish couple who lived there for a good few years before moving back to Ireland. They were very friendly with a friend of hers who now lived in Cricklewood. As far as she knew they were still in touch. This lady introduced herself as Joan Reilly and offered to bring Adam to see her.

When they knocked at the door of No.2 Bells Hill, Cricklewood Joan was pleased to see that her friend Nora Cassidy was in. She gave them a warm Irish welcome. Adam explained to Nora that he had lost his son recently and he was trying to contact some of his old school friends. He explained that the name David Keown had come up. Both women were very sympathetic and pleased to be able to help. Nora explained that Mary Keown had been her best friend when they lived in Camden. Her husband James was a civil engineer and they had three children – two girls and boy. The boy David was the youngest. When James died Mary decided to go back to her own people in Ireland. David, who was an accountant, stayed in London. Later he gave up his job and became a priest. "Did he go back to Ireland afterwards?" asked Adam. "No" said Nora, "He is now a curate in St. Justin's in Whitechapel". "Mary herself," Joan explained "is living with cancer. She has had it a good few years now and is putting up a good fight. I hope to go to see her next month" she added. "She lives in Glenroe, Co Derry in Northern Ireland. Her two daughters are married close by which is very nice for her. Father

David comes to see her as often as he can but it is not easy for him because his parish priest is very old and St Justin's is a very poor parish. "Are you a Catholic yourself?" asked Nora. "No, I'm a Jew" said Adam, "but my wife is a Catholic".

Suddenly Nora remembered that she had some recent photographs that Mary had sent her. She went into another room to find them while Adam and Joan chatted. As soon as Adam saw the photographs of David he knew without any doubt that he was his son. 'I must find him soon', he thought. Nora prepared a nice tea for all of them and told Adam that if she could be of any assistance to him in the future she would gladly help. Adam thanked Joan and Nora for the help that they had already given him. He gave each of them his business card and two tickets for a show in the Royal Opera House in Covent Garden which came as a great surprise to them. They had never in all their wildest dreams thought that they could ever afford to go there.

Adam drove Joan home to Cricklewood. When Rachael rang from Carennac a little later Adam sounded in a very good mood indeed but he felt guilty about not sharing his secret with her. He felt that the right time would come and that one

day she would thank him for having waited.

Part Two

The snow was falling softly over White Chapel as Adam Kohn made his way towards St Justin's Church. The place looked like an old English Christmas card and very different from the White Chapel of his youth. He remembered the trips his father had brought him on to funerals of near and distant relatives when he thought the place looked so dismal and derelict. It was here, to Whitechapel, that his father had come from Hamburg after World War 1 and where his ancestors had come to early in the 19th Century. They were skilled craftsmen –tailors, tanners, bakers and metal workers. Adam's father Fritz had a university education so one of his uncles got him a job in the Schofield Banking Co. where he worked his way up to managerial level and married Anna Schofield, the only child of the banks owner. The bank was going down at one point but, thanks to the hard work of Fritz Kohn, they succeeded in keeping it afloat. By the time David Schofield died Fritz and Anna had inherited a lucrative bank. Later, when they had a family of three boys, the bank became known as Kohn and Kohn.

As Adam parked his car in the spacious grounds of the church people were leaving. A service had finished so he assumed that perhaps the Church would be closing. He hurried in. A few people were still inside praying and lighting candles. He asked a woman when would the Church be closing. She replied "Fr David usually closes it at eight o clock when all the people are gone. You still have half an hour".

He sat down and looked around. There was a large plaque on the wall with the notice 'Donations Urgently Needed for A New Roof-Please Help us'. Adam had come well prepared for an event like this as Nora

Cassidy in Cricklewood had told him that St. Justin's in White Chapel was a very poor parish. Adam knew that it would not be easy for Fr David to get back to Ireland to see his Mother when finances were an issue. Soon Fr David appeared out of the sacristy and sat praying on a seat near the alter. Adam went up to the alter and put some money in the collection box. He then handed the priest a bundle of notes and said "this is for your own personal use". Fr David's face lit up with gratitude! As Adam looked into the brown eyes of his long lost son and held the hand he had so lovingly stretched out to him a verse of poetry came into his head from his English class in Eton so long ago. It was a line from one of WB Yeats poems. He could not remember the poem or the context in which it was used but he did remember the words so well - 'A terrible beauty is born'. He said goodbye to Fr David and made his way to the car. The snow was still falling. A little robin had hopped on the bonnet of his car. He wondered if this was a good omen. He had found what he had set out to achieve - to find a son who would be good to his wife. He would think no more about an heir to Kohn and Kohn. That he would leave in the lap of the gods.

A month went by and Adam decided to pay another visit to St Justin's Church. All the snow had gone and he was able to see the roof. It was indeed in a very bad state he thought. Some repairs had been done over the years which resulted in slates being replaced by other slates that weren't quite the same. It definitely needed a whole new roof. He wondered if the timber beneath the slates was alright. Adam decided that he must give them more help. When he entered the Church he found Fr David there on the his own preparing the alter for the next service. He sat down on a seat. When Fr David had finished he came down to talk to him. He told Adam that his dear Mother had died in Ireland and because of the gift of money that he had given to him on his previous visit to the Church he was able to pay a supply priest and go to Ireland for the week before she died. "She died in my arms" he said. This made Adam very happy to be able to do so much for his son. He had already written a substantial cheque for the new roof fund which he handed to him. Fr David was shocked when he read the amount on it. "Are you a new parishioner?" he asked. "I have only seen you here twice and on both occasions you have been very generous".

"No" said Adam "I am not a parishioner, I am not even a Catholic but of the Jewish faith. My wife is a Catholic. We lost our son recently. She had agreed to have him brought up in the Jewish faith so I feel that I owe the Catholic church a favour for my wife's sake". Fr David was very touched. He told him that he was going into the priest's house after he closed the church to have a cup of tea with his parish priest who was always referred to in White Chapel as 'The Padre'. He asked Adam if he would like to join him and assured him that the Padre would be very pleased indeed to see a cheque of this enormity going into the parish roof fund. "He doesn't often see this much money in White Chapel" he added.

Adam accepted the invitation and soon they were tucking into a nice supper in the priest's house. The Padre, who introduced himself ad Fr Leon Casey, gave him a warm welcome. He was an Irishman who had spent many years as chaplain in the British Army and was stationed in many places in Europe during World War 1. It was while he was in France after the war that he got the name Padre. When he looked at the cheque he was shocked at what he saw. All he could say was "Boys, Oh Boys!" Adam was bemused. He had never heard that expression before. Fr David explained that it was an old Irish expression but not used much even in Ireland today. When Adam mentioned that his wife was French the Padre was very interested. He had met a Frenchman, Pierre Martin, in the trenches during World War 1 and had become very friendly with him. Pierre had promised to take him to France when the war was over. Sadly, it never happened. "He died in my arms in that beastly mud filled trench in Loos in Belgium and I was spared. I went to see his wife in France when the war was over. She lived in the little village of Carennac in the Dordoigne and I loved it so much that I stayed a whole year".

"I don't believe what I am hearing" said Adam. "My wife is from Carennac too! I must arrange for you to meet Rachael soon - you will have so much to talk about". After a while they got around to discussing the roof. Adam asked why the roof was in such a bad state when the main building seemed to be sound. The Padre explained that the original slates were of excellent quality but the workmanship was poor. They were put on with nails and not enough overlap allowed with the result that the damp got in over the years. "The beams are now rotten" he added. They talked late into the night and they both felt that they would see much more of each other in the years to come.

Two years have slipped by very quickly and the roof of St Justin's is now in place and looking very well. The damage to the beams was not as bad as they thought so, much to their surprise, there was money left over in the fund. The parishioners still kept putting money into it and so did Adam Kohn. The Padre was very pleased indeed. He knew that his flock really wanted a parish centre on the grounds of the church but he also knew that it was going to be impossible to get planning permission as the area was too small. He went to the planning authorities again to see if there was anything they could do to find a way around the problem. He found that there wasn't. However, they pointed out to him that there would be space on the grounds for a pre-fabricated hall that may satisfy the needs of the parish and be less expensive. He knew the needs of his parish. The younger people wanted a tea dance every Sunday afternoon while the older generation wanted bingo perhaps a few days a week. Then there were jumble sales and card drives, mother and toddler activities and many more things that were being provided in the other churches in White Chapel. 'Yes' he thought 'a pre-fabricated hall would provide all these things'. He would consult Fr David - he had a good business head being an accountant. Over the years Fr David had been a great help to him. He had looked after the finances of the parish and also took on the duties of a sacristan when they could not pay one. He was very fond of David and knew that he was very lucky to have him as a curate. However, there were times when he sensed that his curate was a lonely man - sometimes he saw a far off look in his eyes and that, coupled with his lack of ambition in the Church, both puzzled and worried the Padre. Both of them had formed a great friendship with Adam and Rachael Kohn and spent many happy days in their home in Regent's Park. Rachael and Fr David had become particularly close. Rachael had become a lukewarm Catholic since she married Adam but now her old faith was coming back and it was a great comfort to her. She often said to Adam that she thought Fr David looked very like what he was when she first met him - the same dark hair and brown eyes that she loved so much. Adam always laughed when she said this and suggested that the Kohns and Keowns were probably the same people a million years ago! She was slowly learning to live without Benjamin but it was hard, very hard at times, on both of them.

Rachael's parents still lived in Carennac and they visited there often. One year they brought the Padre with them to visit his old friends. Pierre's widow Camille was still alive and gave him a great welcome. He was a link with the past for her. She had no family in Carennac. As a matter of fact, she had no living relatives at all now so the Padre had become very special to her. During the visit she asked if there was any help that she could give him as she had inherited money both from her own and Pierre's family. She had helped him in the past with the roof fund. When he mentioned the new hall she said she would help him gladly. The Padre got the impression that Camille was rich. The holiday came to an end too quickly but he would never forget that halcyon summer in Carennac.

When he returned to White Chapel he discovered that Fr David had decorated his room and brightened it up with a beautiful hand stitched patchwork quilt in a colonial design which he had inherited from his mother in Ireland. The Padre was very touched. He assured Fr David that he would always treasure it. Fr David had also bought a few pieces of antique furniture for the priest's house with the money he got from the sale of his Mother's house in Glenroe. The priest's house looked very good now the Padre thought. He would invite Camille to White Chapel. She had never been to London - as a matter of fact she had never been outside of France so he felt that she would enjoy the visit especially as she had struck up a friendship with Rachael Kohn while they were in Carennac. They would be company for each other, he thought.

In the meantime, he pressed on with preparations for the parish hall. Fr David brought him catalogues from different firms which showed a great variety of design. One was very expensive but the Padre liked it very much and hoped that they would be able to buy it. However, he knew in his heart that there was a possibility that they may not. While pouring over the catalogues one day with Fr David a letter was dropped on the floor of the hall. It was for the Padre from Camille thanking him for his kind invitation to London and saying that she would be very pleased to accept. She enclosed a cheque to help with the erection of the new hall. The Padre was shocked when he saw the amount of it. He squeezed Fr David's hand and said "we can afford the most expensive one. Boys oh boys, the parishioners will be pleased!"

Two years have gone by and things are going very well in St. Justin's parish. The new hall is up and running. The tea dances on Sunday afternoons are a money spinner. They are now able to afford to pay a sacristan so that Fr David's workload is not so heavy. Yet the Padre still sees that far off look in his eyes and wonders if Fr David is really happy. They are great friends but when the Padre tries to get closer to him a barrier goes up between them and the Padre feels that he is intruding. He decided he would confide in Camille when she came. 'She is a bubbly person - full of fun - perhaps she will get through to him' he thought.

Summer has come to White Chapel and so has Camille. The Padre always referred to June in England as 'the month of the roses'. The grounds of the priest's house are beautifully laid out with rose beds thanks to the enthusiasm and hard work of Fr David who spent every single spare moment of his life in the garden. Camille was also a very keen gardener and very soon they were bosom friends. Fr David had never been to France - he had gone to Ireland for all his holidays while his mother was alive. This year Camille insisted that he come to France and stay with her explaining that Carennac looked best in the autumn. Fr David said he would love to. Who could refuse Camille's bewitching smile? Fr Jean Tremblay, who was their supply priest, knew the Dordoigne and told Fr David that it was like New England in the fall. When Fr David told the Padre of the invite he was delighted - Camille was obviously getting through to him. Camille and the Padre were having a great time together too. He brought her to see anything that was worth seeing in London. They went on boat trips on the Thames, walked along the serpentine and went for long walks on Hampstead Heath. It was while they were sitting at the pond in Hampstead village after a very invigorating walk on the heath that the Padre dropped a bombshell. "Camille", he said "I am still in love with you. I have felt this way since I first met you in Carennac in 1918. You were grieving for Pierre then so it wasn't the time to tell you. My love for you was the reason why I stayed in Carennac a whole year and it was because of my love for you that I decided to go back to England because I had nothing to offer you. I have regretted this decision ever since".

"Oh Leon, why didn't you tell me?" sobbed Camille. "I have lived for your letters all these years and I still love you as you love me". They held hands and kissed. At seventy six they both knew they were not too old for love. They had both loved and lost and found love again - this time forever they hoped.

When they returned to St. Justin's Fr David had a lovely supper prepared for them and noticed that they were very happy. Camille was delighted to talk about Hampstead Village and the Pond - the highest spot in London as she had learned. Fr David knew it of old but said no more. Camille thought she detected a sadness in his eyes but she too kept silent. Later on she mentioned this to the Padre who told her that he too, on many occasions, had detected a sadness and had come to the conclusion that Fr David had a secret. "Perhaps he has loved and lost as we have," said Camille. "Let's hope he can find love again" said the Padre as he hugged and kissed her goodnight.

Camille returned to France and both the Padre and Fr David missed her very much. One evening as they sat watching television the Padre surprised Fr David by announcing that he was going to retire soon. He had always imagined the Padre staying on in his job until he dropped dead. He said he would like to go in the next year and retire to Carennac. Camille was lonely and they would be good company for each other. Fr David was indeed very surprised but said no more. 'Could this have been an old romance?' he wondered. Later on the Padre asked him if he would be interested in becoming the new parish priest. A definite 'no' was the answer. "Can I ask why?" said the Padre, "you have done Trojan work while in this parish and I can think of no one more suitable for the position of parish priest". Fr David paused for a moment before he spoke and when he did speak the Padre knew that he had got through to him at last. His exact words were "Padre, I entered the priesthood for the wrong reason and there isn't a day goes by that I don't think of leaving". Then he added "when you retire I will give the matter more thought". The Padre replied "I will keep you in my prayers David, God bless you".

Weeks and months went by and neither of them spoke about their hopes for the future but the Padre noticed a change in Fr David. He seemed more settled and would appear to have lost that faraway look in his eyes. 'Had he come to a decision?' he wondered. As for the Padre himself he had already made his decision. It was now almost Christmas and he had decided to retire in early spring. His impending resignation would remain a secret until then.

One evening in mid-December Fr David called on Rachael Kohn and poured out his heart to her. They had become very close in the past year. It was nearing Christmas and that particular evening Rachael was alone and feeling very nostalgic thinking about Benjamin who had died on Christmas Eve five years ago. They prayed for a little while before Fr David dropped a bombshell. "Rachael" he said "I have been unhappy in the priesthood for a very long time and I am thinking of leaving".

Rachael was shocked. She couldn't believe what she was hearing. "But you are such a good priest David" she said. "I have come back to my faith because of my friendship with you. I hope you have given it enough thought". "Yes, I have" David replied. "It is kind of you to say that I am a good priest but the truth is Rachael that I am not good enough. You see, I entered the priesthood for the wrong reasons and there is not a day goes by that I don't regret it. I once loved a girl - she was the love of my life - and through my own fault I let her slip away. She has faded into the mists of history but still remains in my mind and heart and will always be part of me".

"I am so sorry to hear this story" said Rachael. "I wish Adam were here. He has such a good head on him; perhaps he could give you some of his wisdom. I feel that my words are so inadequate". "Don't ever think that" said David. "Talking to you has helped me a lot. I don't get a chance to talk to many women. I was very close to my mother and it was because of her that I decided to part with my girlfriend and enter the priesthood. It was a bad decision - I know that now" he said.

Just with that Adam entered the room. He was delighted to see Fr David and both Rachael and David were very pleased indeed to see him. After tea Rachael plucked up the courage to tell Adam that Fr David had confided in her with a problem that perhaps he was in a better position to advise on. Adam was also shocked when he heard what Fr David had to say. He explained to Adam that the girl he loved was Jewish and that her parents didn't approve of him because he was a Catholic and from an Irish background. "They made life very difficult for Miriam and myself" he added. Adam's eyes lit up when he heard the name 'Miriam'. He cast his mind back to a park bench at Green Park station and a homeless man who told him that his wife was going to be well looked after by his son and a girl called Miriam. Fr David proceeded to explain that he brought Miriam to see his mother in Northern Ireland. She lived in the beautiful town of Glenroe at the foot of the Sperrin mountains. They had a wonderful holiday - walking, cycling and swimming. The weather was lovely and the people so warm, friendly and welcoming. They loved canoeing on the river Roe and as they made love in the long grass at Swan's Bridge they vowed never to part. The world was their oyster they thought. They were happy that David's mother was happy for them.

One evening towards the end of their holiday David found his mother crying. She had been out with some friends all day and he wondered had something happened to upset her. She didn't want to tell him but in the end she blurted it out. Her friends weren't pleased that her son was marrying a Jewish girl. They even said some very nasty things about Jews. She pointed out to him that these were a people who were finding it hard enough to have to cope with the marriage of a Catholic and a Protestant but the idea of a Catholic and a Jew abhorred them. At that moment David realised that he was in Northern Ireland. He knew that his mother was going to have to live with these people for the rest of her life. After all they were her own people and she loved them. Miriam and himself talked about the situation late into the night. Their hearts were broken. It was bad enough to have Miriam's family turn against them; they couldn't break David's mother's heart as well. Their marriage couldn't be blessed, they thought. Next day they returned to London with tears in their eyes and after a final kiss at the pond in Hampstead Village they parted. David knew that he would never love again so after a year or two he decided to give his life to God. That would please his mother very much. It was a bad decision. "I have regretted it ever since" David added.

Adam didn't speak for a while until he recovered from the shock of what he had just heard. At last he spoke out bluntly. "Fr David, you must leave the Church at once if you are not happy there. You are a chartered accountant and as you know there are many jobs in the city. That is my advice to you and it is given in all sincerity as if you were my son. Fr David thanked him for the advice and added that he appreciated both his friendship and Rachael's very much. Rachael was surprised that Adam was so blunt but she was in for a bigger surprise a little while later when she returned to the room with fresh coffee to discover that Adam had offered Fr David a job at Kohn and Kohn! He gave him a month to make up his mind. Later when Adam and Rachael were alone Rachael broached the subject again. "Adam, you must really like David to have offered him a job" she said. "Yes I do" Adam replied. "He has a good business head and will be a great asset to Kohn and Kohn. You like him too, don't you?" he asked. "Yes I do, very much" said Rachael, "but that is because I think he is so much like you!" she said with a giggle as she hugged and kissed him goodnight.

As Fr David made his way home to the priest's house his mind was made up. He was going to accept the job that Adam had offered him. He was now thirty-five and young enough to start a new career he thought. He would confide in the Padre as soon as he got home.

When he entered the hall he found the Padre sitting on the stairs sobbing his heart out. His face was ashen white and there was a tremor in his hand. Fr David took the telegram he was holding and read it. It was from a friend of Camille's in Carennac to say that Camille had died peacefully in her sleep that morning. Funeral arrangements later. Fr David prayed with him and gave him any words of comfort that he could but he was inconsolable. They both knew that life ahead was going to be lonely. Needless to say David did not burden the Padre with any of his own problems.

Adam and Rachael brought the Padre to Carennac for the funeral. Camille was very popular in the village where she lived all her life so the funeral was well attended. The Padre was heartbroken and Adam and Rachael feared that he would never get over his grief. He was obviously very fond of her. They didn't know, of course, that he had intended to spend the rest of his life with her. After the funeral a gentleman who introduced himself as Camille's solicitor asked them to come with him to her home for the reading of the will. The Padre was very surprised to discover that Adam was the executor of her will. When the solicitor read the contents of the will it came as a shock to all of them. The Padre asked for a glass of water when he discovered that he had become a multi-millionaire! No one expected this as Camille was such a humble little person but the solicitor explained that recently she had inherited money from property which she invested wisely. He added that she had been very lucky on the stock market. When he recovered from the shock the Padre announced that he had a secret wish and that he was going to fulfil his dreams by doing something worthwhile in Camille's memory.

Next day they returned to London. On the journey back he seemed more placid and he confided in Adam and Rachael that his secret wish had been to build a hostel for the homeless men of Whitechapel and beyond. The nuns had provided shelter for homeless women for years but many men were still sleeping rough. Adam was very interested and told him that when the time came he would bring him to meet an old friend of his who helped to run a hostel in Abbey Street who he hoped would give him some good advice. Of course they all agreed that getting a suitable site was going to be the problem.

A month had gone by and David Keown has joined Kohn and Kohn bank and a new curate has arrived in St. Justin's. When the Padre opened the door in answer to his ring he couldn't believe his eyes when he saw him. He had long hair almost to his shoulder, drain-pipe trousers and shoes with pointed toes. In a broad cockney accent he introduced himself as Fr Daniel Boyle. The Padre gave him a warm handshake and said he was glad to welcome a fellow Irishman. However, Fr Daniel was very quick to correct him announcing that he was an English Boyle. He explained that his ancestors did not come from Ireland after the potato famine. "However", he said "it's a long story and I will tell you all about it later on. In the meantime I'm dying for a cup of tea. I'll put on the kettle myself if you show me where the kitchen is". The Padre was highly bemused. He wasn't used to a colourful character like this as curate but for some strange reason he liked him. In the weeks ahead he was to grow to like him even more. When they had finished tea they retreated to the sitting room where Fr Daniel expected to be given a list of his duties and a sermon on the do's and don'ts of the parish but to his surprise the Padre appeared to only want a cosy little chat. "Now tell me about yourself and these English Boyles that you say you belong to. You see my Grandmother was a Boyle and I always thought that my ancestors were Irish. I am very interested in genealogy and I have a feeling that you and I are going to get along fine". This pleased Fr Daniel very much. He felt he was off to a good start.

He proceeded to explain to the Padre that the information he had was handed down by word of mouth. He said that he was given to understand that his father line was Pretani and that his ancestors were the very first inhabitants of Britain who were driven out by the Anglo-Saxon invaders of the 5th and 6th Century. Some settled in Scotland and were later known as the Picts. "And you, Padre, are stuck with one of them!" joked Fr Daniel. "Well boys oh boys, I've heard of an Irishman Columba who didn't get on very well with the Picts" said the Padre. "And I heard of an Englishman 'The Venerable Bede' who called the Picts an abomination" came Fr. Daniels retort.

Just with that Lizzie, the new housekeeper, appeared in the doorway to announce that dinner was ready. Fr Daniel got a surprise when he discovered that they had a housekeeper - he hadn't been used to this in any other parish. But his surprise was nothing compared to the shock Lizzie got when she was introduced to the new curate with a bead in his nose!

Sunday came and the parishioners welcomed him with a handshake outside the church after mass. He had preached a very interesting sermon which went down well with young and old. He wasn't going to be a 'happy clappy' priest they felt, but his sermon showed that he had a great sense of humour which appealed to them. Later in the afternoon he joined the young people at the tea dance in the hall and thoroughly enjoyed himself. When he joined the Padre later for dinner Fr Daniel mentioned that he noticed that most of the dancers were Irish. "Yes" said the Padre "we don't seem to attract the Poles and the English. We have a problem there and I don't know how to put things right". "Leave it with me" said Fr Daniel. "I think the problem is with the music. We are living in the seventies but the music and dances are of the fifties. I notice that you have turntables, an amplifier and speakers but no disco dancing. I was a DJ before I became a priest and I would be very pleased to try my hand at it again if you give me permission" Fr Daniel added. "Will we try it next Sunday?" he asked.

"Of course I will give you permission if you think that will attract more young people" said the Padre delighted with the suggestion. "However, I think a one-hour session will be enough to start with - I don't want to lose the middle aged people who have been coming to the hall from the very beginning. But I'll leave it in your capable hands. I have a gut feeling that you will solve my problem" he added.

Very soon there was another problem to be solved - that of the maintenance of the garden. Fr David had kept it in great shape while he was there because he loved gardening. Sometimes the Padre thought that he was working to calm his nerves and now, in the light of recent events, he felt his suspicions were correct. Fr Daniel confessed that he knew nothing about gardening. The Padre confided in him that he had recently inherited some money of his own and that he was thinking of employing a gardener a few days a week. Fr Daniel didn't approve. "It will cost too much" he said. "If you leave it to me I will think of something. You shouldn't have to spend any of your own money on a project like this - keep it for bigger things" said Fr Daniel. The Padre smiled and with a twinkle in his eyes asked him how he knew that there were 'bigger things'. Before Fr Daniel had time to answer the Padre blurted out his secret wish. They both agreed that it was a very good idea but that procuring a suitable site was going to be a very big problem. As for Fr Daniel, he was only one week in the job and already he had three problems to solve but somehow he felt that they would soon be solved.

The answer to his second problem came to him one night in his sleep. He would consult the Padre next day. When he came down to breakfast Lizzie, the housekeeper, had already told him that she'd heard the tea-dance the previous Sunday was a great success. This gave Fr Daniel confidence to approach the Padre. But when the latter came for breakfast he told Fr Daniel that he had already had a complaint that the music on Sunday was too loud. The problem wasn't quite solved.

When he introduced his plan for the garden the Padre was most impressed. He proposed leasing the twelve flower beds around the church to parishioners for a nominal sum to start a competition. The money raised from the rent could be used for prizes twice a year in Spring and Autumn. That would ensure that the garden would always be well kept. This proposal was very acceptable to the Padre and, knowing the competitive nature of his parishioners, he felt it was going to be a success. He congratulated Fr Daniel saying that he felt that the third problem was safe in his hands. He added "the Venerable Bede may have found the Picts an abomination but the Bishop has sent me one clever one!"

Six months have gone by and the first two problems have been solved. The Poles and English have started coming to the tea-dances greatly enhancing the revenue. One hour of old time dancing has been introduced which has attracted older people as well.

The garden project has been a great success resulting in the gardens being in constant bloom. The Padre is very pleased with how things are going and still hopeful that the third project, his dream, will one day be realised.

One day a fox got into the priest's house and frightened the wits out of Lizzie because she saw him go up the stairs. Fortunately, both the Padre and Fr Daniel were at home and soon got rid of the fox.

The Padre explained that it came from the acre of waste ground behind the church which was known as no man's land. In years gone by they had great trouble with foxes. "Who owns the land?" asked Fr Daniel. "Who knows?" said the Padre, "it probably belongs to the council". Fr Daniel decided to go and see the council the very next day. He discovered that it didn't belong to them - there were no rates being paid on it. He spent days in the archives delving through the land registry only to discover that the land belonged to St Justin's parish. In 1800 the site was bequeathed to them to build a church and this acre was included in the site. It was meant to be for a cemetery but when the wall was built around the church the cemetery, for some reason, was not included. Two World Wars intervened and people forgot the original ownership of the land.

When Fr Daniel entered the priest's house he was waving a piece of paper. He interrupted the Padre in his prayers. "Have I got news for you" he said with excitement. "What is it now?" said the Padre, "are you going to tell me that God is dead and that we are both out of a job?" he joked. "Nothing quite so dramatic!" said Fr Daniel, "but the good news is that no-man's land actually belongs to St Justin's. When he had told the Padre the full story all he could mutter over and over in astonishment was 'Boys oh boys'.

Just with that the doorbell rang and who was standing on the doorstep only Adam Kohn. The Padre was very glad to see him. Their lives had become so intertwined that he was pleased Adam was there to share the special moment with him. Adam pointed out to him that there may be a long drawn out legal procedure because of the length of time the land had been vacant. He said he would give him all the help he could when the time came. He also mentioned his friends who ran the men's hostel in Abbey Street. Adam would introduce them to the Padre when the time came and he felt sure that they would be able to give him some sound advice.

David Keown, he informed the Padre, was now in the bank's Dublin branch. He talked of David's promotion and said he felt that he was going to be a great asset to Kohn and Kohn. Adam promised to ring David that very night and tell him the good news about the site the church had unexpectedly acquired.

"Deo gratias" said the Padre, "I will remember you all in my prayers".

Part Three

Another two years have gone by and the building of the hostel is almost completed. The scaffolding has been taken down and the building looks very good. The Padre is delighted. Many obstacles were encountered along the way but they got there in the end. It is now going to be a hostel and parish centre combined and is to be known as the 'Camille Centre'. The parishioners are very pleased. They know that the Padre dug deeply into his own pocket to achieve this and they are very grateful. Their joy knew no bounds when they discovered that they were eligible for a generous government grant to complete the work. "Camille must be looking after us" the Padre said time and time again. He would ask Adam and Rachael to bring him to Carennac to visit her grave. He needed inspiration and he felt that this trip would give him just that. He had many decisions to make in the next few months including the appointment of a manager. He would deal with all these things when he came back he decided

When they returned from Carennac Adam brought him to the hostel in Abbey

Street where Matt Malone is now assistant manager. As luck would have it Matt was in charge that day as Dan Molloy had gone on holidays to Ireland. Matt explained to them that Dan had a house in Donegal and went there twice a year. "His heart is really there" he added. "He hopes to retire there next year. I will miss him very much when the time comes". The Padre was very impressed by the hostel and decided then and there that he would like to give the job to Matt Malone. He knew that Adam would like this and he felt that Adam's judgement was sound. He would ask the local Methodist curate and Fr Daniel to assist him with the interview.

The morning of the interview came and just as the curate of the Methodist church approached the door of the priest's house an ambulance came in the driveway. Two paramedics jumped out in haste. They rang the bell. Fr Daniel appeared in the doorway looking very distressed. Apparently the Padre had fallen down the stairs and was in great pain. The Methodist curate offered his assistance. Both Fr Daniel and himself suspected a broken hip. The paramedics soon made him comfortable in the ambulance and assured him that he was going to be alright. The Padre asked Fr Daniel to accompany him to the hospital which he was only too glad to do. He asked the Methodist curate to interview Matt Malone whispering in his ear that he had come highly recommended and assuring him that he was the one they wanted for the job. As the ambulance drove off the Rev Mattie Malone was bemused by the fact that he was about to interview somebody with a similar name. Lizzie the housekeeper brought him a cup of tea as he sat down to read Mr. Malone's curriculum vitae.

There was a shock in store for him. The words jumped out from the pages. This couldn't be, he thought. He was about to interview his long lost father! Just with that the doorbell rang and he could hear Lizzie ushering the candidate into the front room. Memories came flooding back to him of that terrible day long ago when he ran away from home. He knew that he must have hurt his father by not staying with the woman who was looking after him. Then he remembered that he stole buns and lemonade from a shop. His father would be ashamed of him, he feared. He carried these feeling of guilt with him all his life and now he was going to meet him face to face. Would he ever forgive him? Soon the door opened and Lizzie introduced Mr Matt Malone. Both men stood speechless.

The tragedy of Sohrab and Rustum from Matthew Arnold's poem came flashing through Mattie's mind but it didn't last long. Soon he was in Matt's arms - those strong arms that held him as a child and tried to shield him from all harm after his mother died. "Mattie, I have missed you so much" he said. "I hope that you find it in your heart to forgive me for abandoning you. You see, when I got ill I had no home to offer you and I thought that you would be better in a secure home with somebody else. It took me a long time to get on my feet again. By that time I was afraid you would be ashamed of me".

"Me ashamed of you?" said Mattie. "It is I who should be asking you to forgive me for running away from home and, worse still, for stealing food from a shop. I knew that I had hurt you and I thought that was why you had sent me to a new home. I missed you so much Papa. My dad and mum were very good to me and I still miss them - they died in a car crash in Nigeria two years ago while working as Methodist missionaries there. I will never let you go again" he added.

Matt detected a sadness in his son's eyes when he said this. He wondered if he had said something wrong. Mattie noticed his concern and he immediately tried to put him at his ease. He said "Papa, I have something to tell you that you may not like. Very soon I may be going to Ireland where I have been offered the position of rector in the village of Glenúna in Donegal. I have a girlfriend in Dublin. She is training to be a teacher and we hope to get married in a few years' time. She hopes to get her mother's job and, as her father is the rector in Glenúna, it is his job that I have been offered. He is retiring soon". Matt hugged his son. "I am so proud of you" he said, "and your Mama would be really proud if she could see her little Mattie a man of the cloth. Now tell me about your girlfriend" Matt insisted.

Mattie decided that they would continue their conversation elsewhere suggesting that they go to his place for the evening. "What about the interview?" asked Matt. "Have I got the job?" Mattie replied "I will tell the Padre that I have given you a week to make up your mind and we will leave the final decision in the lap of the Gods".

Later over tea in the Manse Mattie asked his father would he be free to come to Ireland with him in a few days' time. He was planning to go to Glenúna to have a look at the place before accepting the job. "I would love your company Papa" he said. Matt was delighted. "As a matter of fact I will be on holidays next week and I would love to accompany you. Thank you so much for asking me" replied his father. They talked late into the night. It was as if they had never been separated. Theirs, they felt, was going to be a very special bond.

After a few days they flew to Belfast where they hired a car. Soon they were on their way to Glenúna not knowing what to expect. Matt hadn't been on holiday since his wife Gwen had died so this was a real treat for him. Mattie was so happy to be able to do this for his father. When they got within ten miles of Glenúna the scenery got wild and beautiful. Soon Glenúna was in sight - a riverside village in an awe-inspiring landscape. Here at the entrance to the village, near an historic ivy-clad bridge, the Methodist church stood - a grey stone building - very plain but with beautiful white latticed windows. Further up the village they found a Gothic revival church in dark sandstone which they presumed was the Catholic church. The 'Red House' where the Methodist minister resided is overlooking the yellow river near a waterfall where salmon can be seen coming in from the open Atlantic and struggling to get up the river at the salmon leap.

The Red House itself is a solid red brick house unadorned and redeemed from positive plainness without by the Virginia creeper and wisteria of many years' growth climbing its face and now covering it in a mantle of green and red. The gardens are now mature and of low maintenance. It is spring and the banks of the yellow river opposite the house are a mass of bluebells. Matt is ecstatic. It reminds him so much of Llanberis in Wales where he was brought up. "Do you remember Llanberis Mattie" he asked, "the place where your gran lived?" "Yes, I do" said Mattie, "because I left my little aeroplane on the dresser and I never got it back". "You have a good memory son" said Matt. "I remember that too. Your gran died shortly after our visit and we never got back. The following year your mama died and things began to go wrong after that. The rest is history and we won't dwell on it any longer Mattie". "I'm hungry" his father added, "let's go and eat".

After a sumptuous meal in the local McBricin Inn where the soft-spoken, friendly inn keeper supplied them with maps and brochures of the area, they headed towards the bridge and sat on a seat at the entrance to the river walk to study the map. "It is magic here" said Matt. Nothing could be heard only the sound of the river as it made its way to the mighty Atlantic. As they relaxed into the atmosphere birdsong infiltrated the scene and it was so uplifting. A lark perched itself on a rooftop nearby and they listened in silence to his song in the clear air.

Mattie noticed tears in his father's eyes. Matt explained to him that this place reminded him of the place at the foot of CaderIdris where he so often came with Gwen in their courting days. It was here that he proposed to her and they vowed never to part. "Mattie" he said, "never let the love of your young heart slip away because you may wander the world and never find what you lost. Take this job if it is what Megan wants" he added. "Yes, it is what she wants" Mattie replied, "but there is something that both of us want very much. We discussed it on the phone last night. Will you come with us to Glenúna and make your home here? We would both love that". Matt's face lit up. He couldn't imagine anything he wanted more than that invitation. "Yes of course I'll come with you!" he said as he hugged his son and listened to the sweet song of the lark in the nearby tree.

Soon it began to feel chilly so they retreated to the inn where they intended to stay the night. While Mattie was making a phone call to Megan to give her the good news, Matt popped into the bar which was now quite crowded. Soon he heard his name being called. He turned around to find his old friend Pete Sweeney who worked with him on the Isle of Grain in the 1950's. "What brings you to this neck of the woods" asked Sweeney. Matt explained that he was here for a few days with his son on holidays. Just as they were talking Mattie appeared in the door in his grey suit, blue shirt and round collar. Pete Sweeney then remembered that Matt Malone was a Methodist and he said "well done Matt".

They talked about the old days on the Isle of Grain. Matt mentioned to him that the only one of the old gang that he was in touch with was Dan Molloy adding that he was now working with him in London. Pete informed him that he was talking to Dan Molloy only the previous week there in the inn. When Mattie joined them for a drink it became quite obvious to him that his father had found a second home in Ireland. They talked late into the night. Mattie told his father that Megan was very happy about their decision. Her parents were on holidays in Canada and they too were very pleased and hoped to come to see them in London on the way back. Mattie added that Megan and himself would become officially engaged then. Matt could see that his son was blissfully happy. That was something that he had never dreamt of seeing.

When news reached Adam that Matt Malone had found his long lost son he decided to go to see the Padre who was still in hospital making a slow recovery from his operation. He found him in good spirits and very pleased to see him. He told Adam that he was highly bemused by the fact that Matt had found his son in the priest's house in Whitechapel. Adam remained completely silent which was out of character for him.

This puzzled the Padre. He felt that Adam had something on his mind that he wanted to tell him. At last he blurted it out. "Padre" said Adam, "would it surprise you to learn that I too have found my long lost son in exactly the same place? Well, not exactly the same place - I found my son in St. Justin's church". The Padre was very confused. "But Adam" he said, "I thought your son had died". Gradually the story unfolded. The Padre couldn't believe what he was hearing. At last Adam plucked up the courage to ask him for forgiveness. "My friend" he said, "I have deceived you for the past few years by not telling you the whole story from the start. Rachael still doesn't know. I thought that if I told her when she was grieving that it would hurt her even more. I am hoping that both of you will find it in your hearts to forgive me". "Of course I'll forgive you" said the Padre, "and I am sure that Rachael will too. Boys oh boys, that's some story indeed".

Adam was in a very pensive mood as he drove home to Regent's Park. He was going to tell Rachael his secret that very evening and he hoped that she would forgive him as the Padre had done. She was in the kitchen preparing dinner. He gave her a hug and as she looked up at him she noticed that he looked worried. He appeared to have something on his mind. "Adam" she said, "are you feeling alright?". He assured her that he was just fine but that there was something he wanted to tell her. "I want to ask your forgiveness for deceiving you for the past few years" he said. "Oh Adam, you didn't have an affair, did you?" she asked. Adam was shocked but glad he didn't have to confess anything along those lines. "No! Of course I didn't have an affair" he said. "Tomorrow I will bring you to our little garden at Green Park station and I will tell you my secret". "Let me guess" said Rachael, "Kohn and Kohn are going down in business and you have had financial worries that you didn't tell me about". "No, nothing like that" said Adam "what I have to tell you is something that will please you". "Then why do you have to ask for my forgiveness" asked Rachael. "Have patience with me until tomorrow" Adam urged "and then you will understand all and I am hoping that you will forgive me". As he hugged and kissed her he knew that everything was going to be alright.

While they were having dinner Adam mentioned casually that David Keown was coming back from Dublin to the London branch. "You liked David, didn't you?" Adam asked. Rachael detected a twinkle in his eyes. "Yes, I did" said Rachael and just at that moment she suspected that Adam was jealous - that he thought she was in love with David and that was why he had been sent to the Dublin branch. "Adam" she pleaded, "I only liked David because he was so much like you with those brown eyes and black hair. You know that it is you I have always loved". Adam took her in his arms and kissed her. He had to finally reveal the truth. "Yes" he said, "David is like me Rachael because he is our son". There was complete silence for a moment. The secret was out but Rachael couldn't quite take it in. At last she said "Adam, how long have you known this?". "A few years" said Adam. "You were grieving for Benjamin so I thought that it wasn't a good time to tell you," he added. "So that is why you hoped for my forgiveness" said Rachael. "Oh Adam, you know that there is nothing to forgive" she added. "If you had told me then I would not have been able to accept it".

"Do you remember the little slip of paper that fell out of the trunk when we fetched Benjamin's baby clothes?" Adam asked. "Yes, Mary Keown's address" replied Rachael. "I detected a similarity in the names Kohn and Keown so I followed my lead. Soon I was to discover that my long lost son was a Catholic priest in a poor parish in Whitechapel. I was stunned to be honest. However, when I visited the church and met him my feelings changed. I saw myself and I wanted to help him. The rest is history" said Adam.

They talked long into the night. How would they break the news to David? Would he accept his new status? After all he was now the heir to Kohn and Kohn and he may not want the responsibility. Adam further explained to Rachael that when he set out to find his son what he was really looking for was someone who would look after her but when he discovered that he was a Catholic priest he learned something about himself. He was as bad as his brothers. What he really wanted was an heir to Kohn and Kohn. However, when he met David, all these thoughts vanished. He knew that he was the one that would look after her and that was all that mattered.

Next morning Rachael decided that instead of going to the garden at Green Park station she would prefer to go to the pond in Hampstead village where they brought Benjamin so often to feed the ducks. Adam agreed knowing that she was still grieving. She had tossed and turned in the bed all night and he knew that the shock of his news the previous day was bearing heavily on her. He knew that he was going to have to keep an eye on her in the next few weeks.

They took the tube to Hampstead and walked slowly up the hill to the pond. The place was so full of memories for both of them. They stopped at a little café near the pond for morning coffee. It was a very hot day so they decided to sit outside. The chairs all appeared to be occupied but, as they were about to look for seats inside, two ladies beckoned to them that there was room at their table. They assured them that they were just waiting for their husbands and children and would be going soon. Adam and Rachael thanked them most sincerely. They introduced themselves as Moira and Úna Lynch. Rachael said she thought they looked very familiar. Moira said that they were twin sisters over from Northern Ireland for the weekend and having a girly day out. They were married to brothers who had taken the children off their hands for the morning. After a little while they were joined by their husbands and two boisterous children with red hair. Rachael got very upset and broke down in tears. These boys, she explained to them, were the spitting image of her own son Benjamin who had died some years back. Adam tried to console her as best he could but had to admit that the similarities were uncanny.

The visitors were very sympathetic and offered words of great comfort to Rachael. Adam offered to buy an ice cream for everybody and who could refuse such an offer on a hot day in Hampstead? The boys were ecstatic. One boy was called David. Rachael mentioned that she knew a David also.

Just then who appeared walking towards them only David Keown! He got the shock of his life when he saw Adam and Rachael. He explained to them that these were his family from Glenroe in Northern

Ireland. He had arranged to meet them here in Hampstead an hour earlier but was delayed. He was glad to find them still there. It was a very warm reunion. It was obvious to Adam and Rachael that David was very fond of his sisters and that his love was returned. How were they going to break this news that they had so closely guarded? Worse still, how was he going to tell the story to his sisters? By tomorrow they felt that all would be revealed. These were the thoughts going through Adam and Rachael's minds as they said goodbye and whispered to David that they hoped to see him very soon.

David didn't come to see them for another week as he was busy house hunting. Rachael was in the garden when he did come and he offered to help her with the weeding. Soon Adam arrived with plants from the garden centre and was very pleased to see him and ask his advice about planting them. Over afternoon tea they discussed what should be done with the garden as it had got neglected recently. David suggested that they pull down some of the ivy in front of the house as it was getting too heavy. "If you tell me where the ladder is I'll try doing a little bit now" he said. Soon some branches were removed and there they discovered the name 'Valhalla' which would appear to have been the original name of the house. Rachael was very excited and informed them that she would use that name in future on her stationary. "It's as if a new phase in my life is about to begin" she said. "Yes Rachael, a new phase in all our lives is about to begin" added Adam.

"Sit down David and brace yourself for some very big news" Adam said nervously. David sat down in a state of shock. "What is it Adam?" he said, "are you ill?". "No, nothing like that" said Adam. "As a matter of fact I am feeling happier now than I have been for years. David, this may be difficult for you to comprehend, but you are our son. You are not a Keown but a Kohn". David sat motionless. Soon the whole story unfolded. Rachael sat crying and holding her son's hand.

There was a long silence that was broken only by David asking Adam how long he had known. Adam replied that he knew for certain from the first evening that he came to St. Justin's and gave him a donation for the roof fund. "And you never told me!" exclaimed David. Rachael said "he told the Padre before he told me". "Let me guess" said David, "all he said was boys oh boys!". Rachael made another pot of tea and they arranged that David would stay for dinner. They talked late into the night and as he kissed them goodnight Adam knew that all was forgiven.

As he drove to his apartment David realised that he was now heir to Kohn and Kohn bank. This would bring responsibilities. Adam and Rachael were now his foremost concern. He also had to break this news to his sisters Moira and Úna in Glenroe. They would be devastated. He recalled the sad day so long ago when he found his mother crying because of nasty things that her friends said to her about Jews. Now his sisters would have to break the news to those same people that their brother was brought up in the Jewish faith and died a Jew. Life can be so cruel in some insular societies he thought to himself. He had a week's leave due so he decided to go to see them. He hoped that this gesture would soften the blow. They would always remain his sisters he hoped.

Part Four

Two years have passed very quickly and it is Spring again in London. The gardens of Valhalla in Regent's Park are ablaze with colour. The yellow, white and blues of the spring bulbs are joined by masses of pink cherry blossom, showy magnolias, rhododendrons, clematis and wisteria. David now lives with Adam and Rachael and spends every spare moment gardening. Rachael likes to take an early morning stroll in the garden and listen to the dawn chorus. She describes the very gentle song of the blackbird as being like the sound of a flute and that of the thrush as being like a flute laughing. She loves this early morning symphony when the birds are at their peak. They fill the air with their songs over and over again. In late evening when she sits in the garden with Adam the sweet song of the nightingale almost lulls them to sleep. David spends a good part of his spare time in the greenhouse preparing his prize roses which he hopes to exhibit at the Chelsea flower show.

One afternoon, when Adam was in town at the board meeting, David arrived home early from work with a message from his Dad. He was going to be delayed at the meeting and wouldn't be home on time to bring Rachael to the Royal Opera House in Covent Garden to hear Pavarotti sing as they had earlier planned. He knew how disappointed she was going to be so he asked David if he would be kind enough to accompany her. "Will you let me bring you?" David asked Rachael. "Of course I will" she replied. "We don't often have the chance of a night out together".

After dinner she dressed in her lime green linen dress which she knew would be cool. David thought she looked radiant and so youthful as she stepped out. He felt so proud of her. With David by her side Rachael didn't want this night to end. He reminded her so much of the Adam of her youth when love was on the wing. She was determined to hold onto this moment and remember it for the rest of her life. As David took her arm they both knew that they were going to enjoy a wonderful evening.

It wasn't quite dark when they emerged from the theatre. David decided to buy a bunch of flowers for his mother from the flower stall at Covent Garden market. He knew her favourites so it wasn't going to take long. Rachael sat down and waited. As David approached the stall he heard his name being called. He turned around and there she was. "Miriam" he shouted, "it has been a long time. How are you?" he asked as he gave her a hug. "I notice you have no round collar David" Miriam replied. "And I notice that you have no ring on your wedding finger Miriam" David replied as he took her hand in a loving gesture. He then asked her to come and meet his mother who at this time was coming to meet them. Miriam was both shocked and puzzled when they were introduced. This was not the mother that she had remembered! David noticed her bewilderment and said "Miriam, it is a long story. I would like to explain it to you sometime if you will let me". "I am free all day tomorrow" replied Miriam as she handed him her business card. As she arranged a beautiful bouquet of flowers for his mother she mentioned that florists never get presents of flowers. "I hope to see you tomorrow '" said David as he kissed her goodnight.

Both David and Rachael were very quiet in the taxi on the way home. Not a word was uttered except to admire the bouquet of flowers that Miriam had made up. At last Rachael plucked up the courage to speak. "Thank you so much David for bringing me out tonight and introducing me to Miriam. She seems such a nice girl. When you go to see her tomorrow bring her that bouquet of flowers that she says florists never get" Rachael said. As he kissed her goodnight Rachael thought that she had never seen David look so happy. She knew Adam would be pleased when he heard this.

Next morning as Rachael took her usual early stroll in the garden she noticed that David was busy in the greenhouse. When he emerged he was carrying a large bouquet of roses that he had just made up.

Rachael was shocked. They were his prize cream roses in bud which he had hoped to exhibit at the Chelsea flower show. "But David" she said, "these are your prize roses. I'm surprised that you are parting with them". Just with that Adam appeared in the doorway. He had overheard the conversation and was highly bemused. "David" he said, "we have Chelsea every year but true love doesn't come often so we have to grasp it with both hands when it does come or it may never come our way again. Go for it!" David blew them both a kiss as he disappeared out the gate.

When David emerged from the tube at Golders Green station he was a bit apprehensive about meeting Mr and Mrs Levy again because their relationship in the past was anything but cordial. He was, in their eyes, the son of an Irish immigrant and Catholic - no way good enough to marry their daughter. He had more confidence now and was determined to win Miriam back. She was in the garden of her old home - obviously still living with her parents - and went to the gate to meet him. He thought she looked radiant in a yellow linen dress which complimented her olive skin and large brown eyes. They were alone in the house when he presented her with the bouquet saying that they were from his own garden. "David" she exclaimed, "they are beautiful. No one had ever given me cream white roses in bud before". Then she read the little card that he had written:

'I send you a cream white rose bud with a flush on its petal tips. For the love that is purest and sweetest had a kiss of desire on the lips'.

Miriam remembered these lines from the Irish poet John Boyle O' Reilly. How could she ever forget them? David had whispered them to her when he asked her to marry him so many moons ago. She looked up at him. Her sweet proud lips were parted in utter surrender and lifted to his. When he kissed her they were both transported in spirit back to Glenroe. They had found love again in the long grass at Swan's bridge. This time they felt that it was forever.

They sat in each other's embrace for a long time. No one spoke. This moment was bliss. At last David broke the silence by saying that he expected her parents to come in at any moment and split them up as they had often done in the past. Miriam didn't speak. There was an eerie silence. When he looked at her face he saw sadness and tears. "David, you don't know!" she said, "my parents died two years ago while on holidays in Cornwall. They crashed into an articulated lorry and were killed instantly. It was in all the papers at the time and I hoped then that you would write to me but you didn't.

"Miriam I am so sorry" was all David could say as he held her closely. "Two years ago I was in our Dublin branch and of course didn't hear. Oh Miriam you must be hurting. We have so much to talk about" he added.

"We certainly do" said Miriam, "and I noticed the name Kohn on the business card you gave me last night. Have you changed your name David?" she asked. "Let's go for something to eat first Miriam" he replied, "and then I will tell you all. I hope our favourite little restaurant is still doing nice lunches".

"Yes they are" she replied, "it's about the only thing around here that hasn't changed. What's it going to be David - roast beef and Yorkshire pudding?" she teased with the mischievous little smile that he always loved. He wrapped his arm around her waist and they walked out the door.

When they arrived at the Blue Bird restaurant they were ushered into a little side room by the very friendly waitress who obviously knew Miriam quite well. What David didn't know was that Miriam owned the restaurant. She decided not to tell him this yet. When the business had come up for sale Miriam couldn't bear the thought of this special place being turned into anything other than a restaurant. She and David had come here so often in days gone by when love was new. This was what had motivated her to purchase it. They settled down to eat and during their meal the story of David's change of life unfolded. Miriam was flabbergasted. Was she really hearing this or was it a dream she asked herself. "So you are really Jewish David" she said, "we could have been married years ago if my parents had known".

"I hate to have to say this to you Miriam and I am hoping that it will not come between us again. I will always be a Catholic. I have changed my name to Kohn but my religion will never change". Miriam took his hand and said "I admire you for that David. Nobody will ever force me to change my religion so why should I change you.". David and Miriam were at peace with each other and the world.

Spring has emerged into summer and summer into autumn. David and Miriam are planning their inter-faith wedding in the garden of Valhalla in Regent's Park. They are enjoying an Indian summer which means that the many annuals and perennials continue their summer display. Fiery salpiglossis with its blue and purple blends will with the yellow, orange and red heavily veined in deeper tints. Fuchsias, chrysanthemums and dahlias continue to provide splashes of colourful flowers. Adam has made a chuppah - the canopy structure present in traditional Jewish weddings - and Rachael covered it with a beautiful white linen cloth embroidered by her mother in Carennac thus paying homage to David's

French heritage. They hoped to be married under this canopy.

They were married by the Padre and his friend Rabbi Levy who was a distant relative of Miriam's. Because she had no parents alive many of her aunts, uncles and cousins rallied around her. David's sisters in Ireland, along with their husbands and children, came and brought along some of their mother's friends who in the past were unkind to David and Miriam. Old wounds were healed and friendships were formed. Adam didn't forget to invite his old friend Matt Malone who came with his son the Reverend Mattie and his wife Megan. The priest said the traditional vows while the Rabbi did the exchange of rings. David and Miriam wrote and said their own vows to each other. They did the Jewish stamping of the glass at the end of the ceremony. The Padre and Rabbi Levy sang a prayer in Hebrew and it brought tears to the eyes of all present. Both of them had been a great help to David and Miriam in their preparation for marriage. When it came to the question of any children that they might have David and Miriam decided that one would have the girls and the other the boys. As David was brought up with girls he decided that he might get on best with girls. So the decision was made. "We will leave it in the lap of the

Gods" said Miriam as she hugged and kissed him. This decision made things very easy for the Padre and Rabbi Levy considering the strict rules of the Jewish faith. If this decision hadn't been reached the marriage might have had to be postponed or rethought.

After the ceremony the wedding party wined, dined and danced into the early hours of the morning. Rachael was very pleased to be able to get to know Moira and Úna who were Benjamin's blood sisters. They invited her to come to visit them in Glenroe. David assured them that Miriam and himself would bring Adam and Rachael

170

to see them soon. Adam enjoyed meeting his old friend Matt Malone and his son Mattie. On hearing that Adam intended to go to Glenroe, a trip to Glenúna was added to his itinerary. They planned this trip for the following spring. "This is going to be a great opportunity to meet everybody again" Rachael said when she heard the plan. She hadn't been to Ireland much except on a few occasions when she accompanied Adam to the Dublin branch of Kohn and Kohn. She looked forward to visiting Glenroe and Glenúna very much indeed. Recently she had been feeling very tired and, at times, unsteady on her feet. She thought that Adam, who is twenty years her senior, was doing a lot better. They were both very pleased that David and Miriam were planning to come to live with them in Regent's Park after their honeymoon. Adam wondered if they too had noticed Rachael's imbalance while walking. He would mention it to them when they came back from Jersey and perhaps together they could persuade her to see a doctor. When they returned Rachael wouldn't listen to any suggestions about going to see a doctor saying that she always walked like that. They decided not to pursue the matter any further. They would let nature take its course.

Winter passed very quickly and soon it was spring again. David is in the greenhouse every spare moment he has hoping that this year he will manage to exhibit his prize roses. They are all looking forward to their trip to Ireland in May.

At last the day has come and they have arrived in Belfast. Adam and Rachael were never in Northern Ireland before. Rachael marvelled at how green everything looked. Adam teased her by saying that this was because it always rained. However, that day was fine as they drove through the beautiful Derry countryside ablaze with colour.

The yellow gorse and rhododendron were in full bloom and they marvelled at how well their colour blended with the earthy brown of turf and moorland. At last they arrived at their hotel in a beautiful country park in Glenroe at the foot of the Sperrin mountains where they received a warm welcome from the hotel staff. After a meal and a rest Moira and Úna Lynch were informed that they had arrived and very soon they came with their families and whisked them off to introduce them to Glenroe. Many of their mother's old friends came to see them. Attitudes had changed in Glenroe about mixed marriages and they had felt remorseful now about the way they had treated them in the past.

Next day Adam and Rachael spent time with Úna and Moira who just wanted to talk about Benjamin. David and Miriam slipped down to Swan's bridge to reminisce. The grass was wet so they couldn't roll about and make love like they used to. Looking about them they felt that nothing had changed. There were no children canoeing on the river Roe as it was too early in the year. There was just meadow, heathland forest and further on the shore a constant, restless mutation of sea, sky and land. They sat in the car and talked about all the changes in their lives that had taken place since they were last there. Gently Miriam took David's hand and said "I have something to tell you David. We are expecting a baby and I think it will be around Christmas time". He was overjoyed and kissed her again and again. As he held her hand he said "Miriam, Swan's bridge will always be a special place in our hearts".

Next day they headed for Glenúna. The weather was still good and they much appreciated the drive through the beautiful Barnes Gap. Unfortunately, Rachael fell asleep in the car and missed that awe-inspiring scenery as they were approaching Glenúna. When they arrived at the McBricin Inn in the centre of the village where they intended to stay they sensed a carnival atmosphere. The sun was setting behind the gothic tower of a church at the top of the street which was packed with cars. The innkeeper gave them a warm Irish welcome. While serving them with a sumptuous salmon dish, for which the inn was renowned, he explained to them that they had chosen a very good day to visit as there was great excitement in the village. He explained that there had been an inter-faith wedding in the Methodist church that afternoon of a local couple who, years ago, had to separate because they were of mixed faiths. They met again many years later and, as times had changed, they were able to marry today and nobody batted an eyelid. Just as they were speaking who appeared in the doorway only a group of the wedding party. This consisted of the Reverend Mattie Malone and his wife Megan, his old friend Matt Malone and, at their heels, the bride and groom who were none other than Dan Molloy - once known on the Isle of Grain as Donegal Dan - and his old sweetheart Iris Watson. They came to welcome them to Glenúna and to invite them to dance in the barn of the Red House later on that evening.

The Kohn's had never been to an event like this so they were very pleased to accept.

The sun was rising like a golden orb over Crann Ceo when the last of the dancers left the Red House barn and all was still. Before they left for home the next day David and Miriam broke the news to their parents that they were expecting a baby. It was the perfect end to a perfect holiday.

Christmas came and so did the Kohn twins - two boys who were named Adam and Benjamin. The family kept the news that Miriam was expecting twins a secret until the very end. When Adam's two uncles

Isaac and Fritz heard the news that they were going to be brought up in the Jewish faith they were so pleased that they signed all their shares in the company over to David in-trust for the boys. When Adam went to see the Padre in the nursing home where he lived to bring him the good news all the Padre could say was "Boys oh boys! It looks as if it is business as usual at Kohn and Kohn!".

Rachael is still very tired but taking a great interest in the twins. David has taken over the garden and Miriam the household duties so Rachael is free to sit in the garden with Adam. Miriam has leased her florist shops so that she can devote her time to three generations of the Kohn family. Adam and Rachael often talk about how lucky they are to have her and David to look after them.

One afternoon, while helping David in the greenhouse, Rachael fell and was in great pain. They rushed her to hospital. They suspected that she may have broken her hip. In hospital they discovered that her hip was badly bruised but not broken. She was in deep shock so they kept her in overnight. During this time, she confided in the medical staff that she suspected that she had had multiple sclerosis for years but kept it from her family. She explained to them that she was a doctor in her youth and joked that she hadn't forgotten everything she had learned. They ran tests and discovered that she was indeed suffering from MS. David was shocked when he heard the news. "Why didn't you tell me Mum?" he asked. She laughed as she replied "you wouldn't have let me to Ireland if you had known! I would have missed that wonderful trip - getting to know Benjamin's family and of course that great barn dance in Glenúna".

Rachael was brought home to Valhalla in a wheelchair. She was in the best of spirits despite not being able to walk. She told her family that she was determined to live life to the full. "I may not be able to walk" she said, "but I can still see the sun rise and set. I can see the birds fly in the blue sky and listen to the dawn chorus". Adam is by her side. His footsteps are now feeble but like hers his heart is still young. They both thank God for the gift of their lives full of laughter and love amongst strife.

Three years have gone by and the twins are now at kindergarten. They are their grandparents pride and joy. London is experiencing a very hot summer and Adam and David sometimes bring Rachael to the garden very early in the morning and place her wheelchair beneath the shade of the Cedar tree. One morning, as she slept in the shade with Adam by her side, a wispy white cloud scurried across the clear blue sky. Rachael woke up. "Benjamin was here!" she said to Adam. He put his arms around her and said "Rachael, you have just had a nice dream". "No" she said, "it wasn't a dream. He spoke to me and said everything turned out very well in the end. I love you Mam". With his arms still around her Adam said "try to stay awake dear because Miriam will be bringing afternoon tea shortly and I know how you love her cream buns". However, Rachael fell asleep again. When David brought the twins from kindergarten they tried to waken her up but didn't succeed. David tried to find a pulse but there wasn't any. She had died. Rachael Kohn, who had given and received so much love all her life had entered the eternal sleep. Her soul had flown to the heaven of the spirits beyond all sorrow and had sought in that great afar the perfect love.

Printed in Great Britain
by Amazon

44282427R00111